It's a Bear's Life

Written by
Anna Wilson

Illustrated by
Suzanne Diederen

MACMILLAN CHILDREN'S BOOKS

Oscar and Parker lived together just like any other boy and bear.
But Parker couldn't help feeling he wasn't a very **lucky** bear.

He liked playing,
but not when it hurt.

Ouch!

Ooo-oo!

He liked being carried,
but not when it was so bumpy.

He liked breakfast, but not when it was so messy.

Yuck!

"AND it's cornflakes again . . .
bears don't even LIKE cornflakes!"

Parker followed Oscar to nursery as usual.

It was painting day – but Parker didn't like painting,
especially when he was the paintbrush.

Later that night, Oscar and Parker had their bath together . . .

and their bedtime story . . .

and their bedtime hug.

"Night-night," said Oscar, sleepily.

Then he rolled over and . . .

BUMP!

"That's it!" Parker cried out.
"I need a break . . . a break from bumps and bruises."

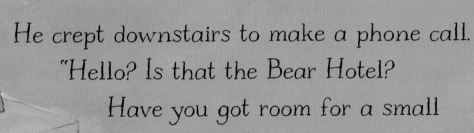

He crept downstairs to make a phone call.
"Hello? Is that the Bear Hotel?
Have you got room for a small
brown bear?"

He packed his bag
as quietly as he could,
and found a pen
to write a note.

Dear Oscar,
Gone on holiday.
Love from
Parker. x

And then he left, closing the front door quietly behind him.

Parker got to the station just in time.
"Move along now, move along," the guard was shouting.
"All aboard the Midnight Growler for the Bear Hotel!"
Parker jostled and pushed his way into the train.

At last he managed to
find a seat and squeezed in
just as the train jolted forward.
Soon he was fast asleep.

He woke up to a delicious smell wafting in through the train window.

"Mmmm . . . honey! PANCAKES and honey!

We're here – and just in time for breakfast," he thought. And he followed the others into the dining room.

Parker looked around. There were bears everywhere: big bears, small bears, tall bears and bald bears. Suddenly Parker felt rather shy.

Then someone noticed him. "Hello, I'm Max. What a great day to arrive. Today's the day the teddy bears have their picnic!"

The sea was warm, and the honey was runny.

"This is the life for a bear!"
thought Parker, as he looked around
at the other bears.

"Come on in!" cried Max.

The bears played in the sea,
but it wasn't **splashy** enough.

They gave each other piggy-back rides,
but it wasn't **bumpy** enough.

They played ball,
but it wasn't **bouncy** enough.

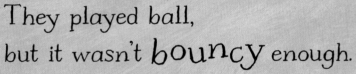

After their games the bears sat on the sand, chatting.
Parker asked them why they had come to the Bear Hotel.

"Oh, my boy's gone on holiday
and left me behind," said one.

"My girl prefers
the company of dolls
these days," said another.

"My boy's too old for bears, and I'm too old for my boy," Max sighed. "What about you?"

"Oh, I – well, I just needed a break," Parker mumbled.

That night the bears didn't have a bath.
They didn't have a bedtime story.
They didn't even have a bedtime hug.

"Night-night," called Parker.
But everyone else was already snoring.

"That's it!" Parker cried out suddenly.
"I miss Oscar! I'm going home."

The Midnight Growler was waiting,
but the guard was surprised to see Parker.
"Going back already, teddy?
All right, all aboard!"

Parker climbed on to the train.
No jostling or pushing this time.
No squeezing or squashing.

Midnight
Growler

Zzzz-Zzzz-Zzzz-Zzzz . . .

Parker stretched out, smiled, and was soon snoozing.

Oscar was asleep when Parker
pushed open the bedroom door.

"Hello, Oscar,"
he said quietly.
"I'm home."

"What's that?"
said Oscar drowsily.
Then he leapt out of bed.

"PARKER!" he shouted, hugging him tightly.
"I've missed you so much! I had no one to play with, no one to
paint with and . . . and . . . oh, don't go away without me again."

Oscar and Parker live together just like any other boy and bear. But now Parker can't help thinking he's a pretty **lucky** bear.

Wee-ee-ee!

Parker likes playing, even if it does hurt a little bit.

Ouch!

Ooo-oo!

Parker likes being carried, even if it is a bit bumpy.

But best of all, Parker likes breakfast, especially when it's . . .